# TREASURE ISLAND

## by ROBERT LOUIS STEVENSON

# #3 On the Island

Adapted by Catherine Nichols

Illustrated by Sally Wern Comport

**Sterling Publishing Co., Inc.**
New York

Library of Congress Cataloging-in-Publication Data Available

10  9  8  7  6  5  4  3  2  1

Published by Sterling Publishing Co., Inc.
387 Park Avenue South, New York, NY 10016
Copyright © 2007 by Sterling Publishing Co., Inc.
Illustrations © 2007 by Sally Wern Comport
Distributed in Canada by Sterling Publishing
c/o Canadian Manda Group, 165 Dufferin Street
Toronto, Ontario, Canada M6K 3H6
Distributed in the United Kingdom by GMC Distribution Services
Castle Place, 166 High Street, Lewes, East Sussex, England BN7 1XU
Distributed in Australia by Capricorn Link (Australia) Pty. Ltd.
P.O. Box 704, Windsor, NSW 2756, Australia

Sterling ISBN-13: 978-1-4027-4119-7
         ISBN-10: 1-4027-4119-7

For information about custom editions, special sales, premium and
corporate purchases, please contact Sterling Special Sales
Department at 800-805-5489 or specialsales@sterlingpub.com.

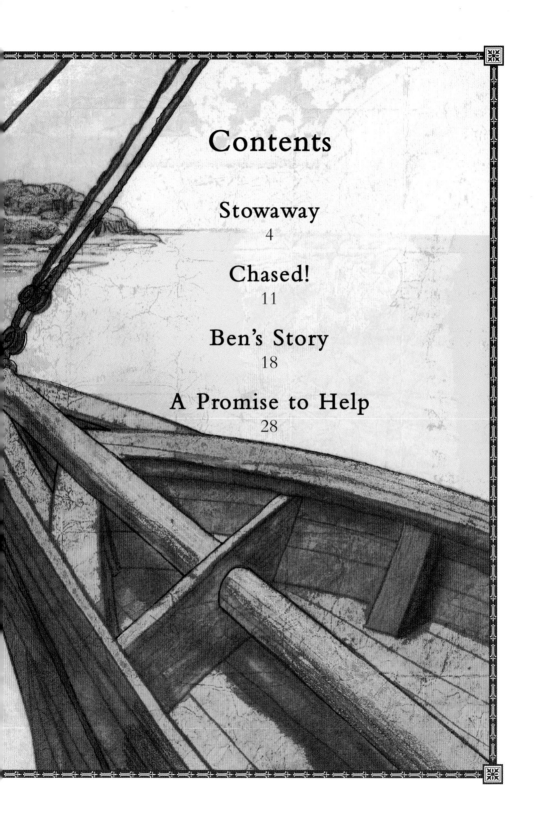

# Contents

## Stowaway

Jim Hawkins was just a small boy,
but he had an important job.
He was a cabin boy
on a big ship.
The ship had sailed
for many days.
Now it had reached
Treasure Island.
Jim and his friends hoped
to find the treasure that
was buried there.

The ship's captain came on deck
with Jim's two friends.
There was Squire Trelawney,
who owned the ship,
and David Livesey, the ship's doctor.
All three men looked worried.
Pirates had hidden on the ship.
They wanted to steal the treasure.

"The pirates want to
take over the ship,"
said the captain.
"But their leader, Long John Silver,
has told them to wait.
He wants us to find
the treasure first."
"What will we do?" asked Jim.
"We have to get them off the ship,"
said the captain.
"And I know how."

He called to the crew.

"No more work!

You have the afternoon off.

Go and explore Treasure Island."

The men cheered.

The pirates got ready
to leave.
Jim watched them.
What would they do
on the island?
What trouble would
they cause?

Jim didn't stop
to think.
He stepped
into a boat.
He hid
under a sail.

He would go
to Treasure Island.
He would spy on the pirates
and report back
to the captain.
But one thing worried him.
Was he being very brave
or very foolish?

## Chased!

Jim's boat reached the island first.

Jim jumped out.

Before anyone saw him,

he ran into the woods.

Jim hid behind a tree.
He could hear the
pirates arguing
about the treasure.

Jim was scared.

What if the pirates found him?

He walked deeper

into the woods.

What a strange island it was!
It was filled
with odd-looking trees,
plants, and creatures.
Jim felt like an explorer!

Then Jim heard a noise.

He turned quickly.

Who was there?

Someone was running
from tree to tree.
The creature was bent over.
Its arms almost touched
the ground.

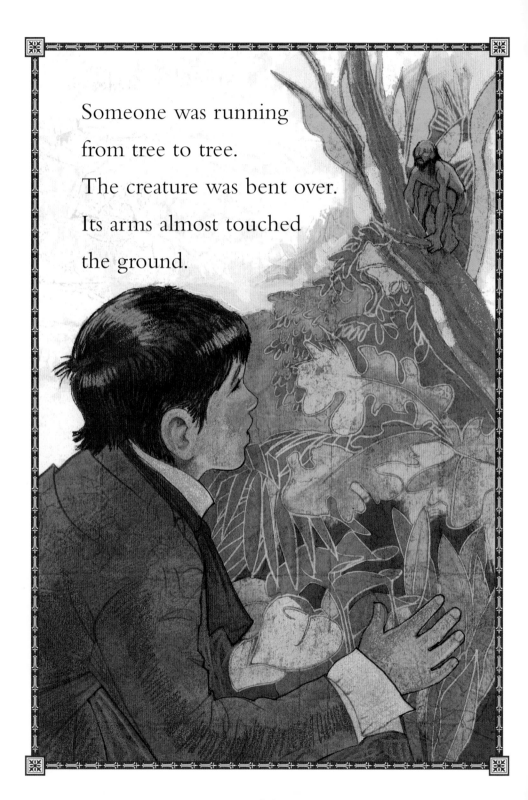

Jim ran.

The creature ran, too!

It was coming after him!

## Ben's Story

Jim was running
toward the pirates.
Wait!
He didn't want
them to see him.
It would be safer
to face the creature!

Jim turned around.

"Who are you?"

he shouted.

The creature fell
on its knees
before Jim.

"I am Ben Gunn," he said.

The creature was a man!

But what a strange-looking man!

His hair was long.

His clothes were rags.

"How did you get here?" Jim asked.

"I came by ship," said Ben.

"I knew treasure was buried here.

My ship's crew came with me.

We looked and looked,

but we didn't find it.

"The crew was angry with me.

One day they left.

They didn't take me.

That was three years ago."

Jim gasped.

Three years was a long time.

No wonder Ben looked

the way he did!

"What do you eat?" Jim asked.

"I eat berries and goat meat," said Ben.

"But I dream of cheese.
Oh, how I would love
some cheese.
Do you have any?"

"No," said Jim.

"But there is cheese
on the ship."

"What ship?"
asked Ben.

So Jim told Ben
all his adventures.
He ended his story
with the pirates.
"They are on this island,"
said Jim.

Just then a cannon fired.
Sounds of fighting
filled the air.
Jim and Ben ran
deeper into the woods.
They hid in a cave.

## A Promise to Help

At last the noise stopped.
It was safe to come out.
"My friends must have
left the ship to fight
the pirates," Jim said.
He wanted to see his friends.
He wanted to make sure
they were all right.
"Look!" said Ben.
Up ahead was a fort.

"Your friends are inside."

"How do you know?"

Jim asked.

Ben pointed to the flag.

It was from the ship.

"If the pirates had won,

they would be flying

their flag," he said.

"Come meet my friends,"
Jim said.

"Tomorrow," Ben said.

"Tonight I'll sleep in my cave.
I feel safer there.

But if you promise
to get me
off this island,
I'll help you
and your friends
fight the pirates.
You have my word."

Jim promised.
He said good-bye
to his new friend.
Then he hurried to the fort.
What adventures he was having!
And tomorrow he was sure
to have more!